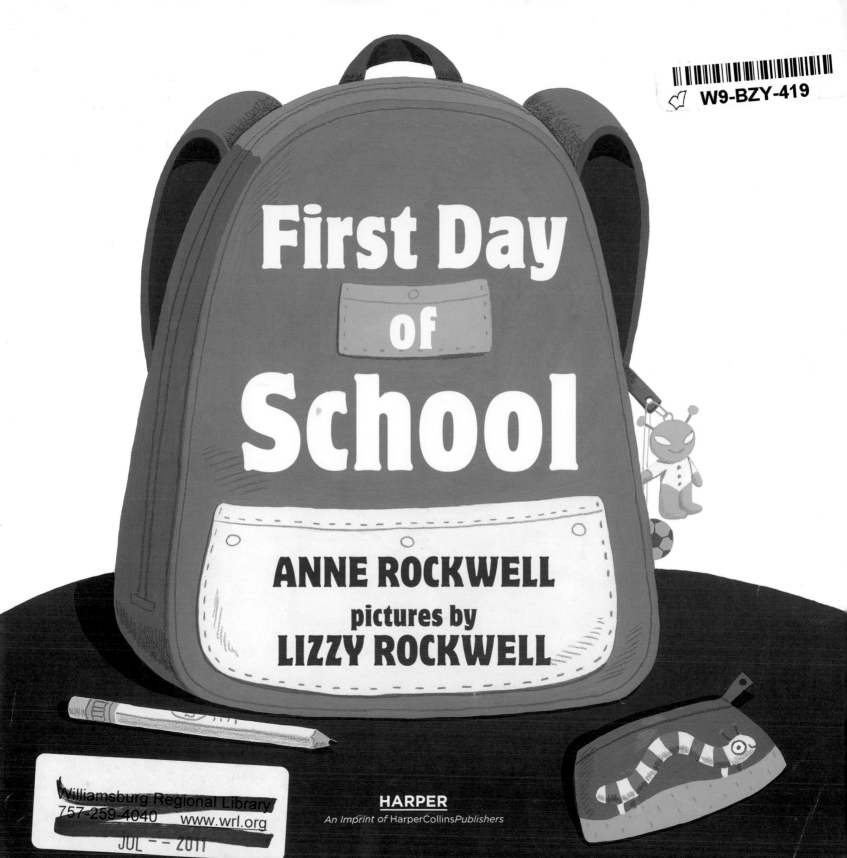

First Day of School

ANNE ROCKWELL

pictures by
LIZZY ROCKWELL

HARPER
An Imprint of HarperCollinsPublishers

Yuck!

When I saw myself in the mirror this morning,

I knew why Mom and Dad said I needed a haircut.

When I drew a picture of myself with my wild

and frizzy hair, Mom and Dad laughed.

But Dad still took me to the barbershop.

After my haircut, I looked so grown up!
"Now I look like you," I said to Dad.
"But you're much more handsome,"
the barber said with a smile.

I asked Dad if we could go to the park.
"Sure," said Dad.

Outside the barbershop,

we bumped into Charlie and his dad.

Charlie was getting a haircut, too.

"See you later," he said.

I hope Charlie is in my class again this year.

We are best friends.

At the park, I saw Sam, Kate, and Sarah.

"Wow! Your hair is so short!" Kate laughed.

"My hair's not too short," I said.

"I want to look good on the first day of school."

"You mean you want to look grown up," said Kate.

"That's right!" I said. "And now I do."

"I bought a new backpack," Kate said.
"At the mall, there were so many to choose from,
I couldn't make up my mind!
Then I saw this one, and it was perfect!
And it was on sale, which made Mom happy, too!"

"Remember our first day of school last year?" Sam asked.

I sure did. It was scary walking down

that long hallway to my classroom.

"I was so scared," said Sam.

"But when Mrs. Madoff showed me where to sit,

I felt better."

"That's because you sat next to me," Sarah said.

"And we were already friends."

"If you guys think you were scared,
you should have seen me!" said Sarah.
"Grandma took me to school early
because she's the crossing guard.
I was the first kid at school!
Only the library was open.
I didn't mind waiting there because
I found my favorite book!"

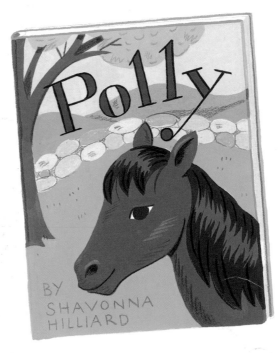

Pablo said, "Last year,
I got a new Captain Dynamo T-shirt.
Remember that one, Nicholas?"
I laughed. How could I forget?
Pablo and I both wore the same T-shirt
on the first day of school!

"Oooh—last year, I wore my beautiful
white dress," said Eveline.
"But it's too short for me,
so Maman made me a new one.
My new dress is white, too, with little
pink roses and a shiny pink belt."

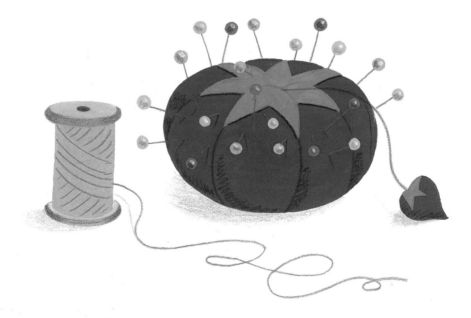

"I can make my own lunch," Jessica said.

"My mom taught me this summer.

I can't wait to use my new Comet Girl lunch box."

"Cool!" said Pablo and Eveline.

"You'll see it tomorrow," Jessica said.

I saw Charlie.

He had a new haircut and a new backpack.

"Let's race to the monkey bars," I said.

Michiko jumped down when she saw us.

"I've got new bouncy shoes!" Michiko said.

"My old shoes were too small.

Now I can wiggle my toes."

I could see all ten toes wiggling inside her shoes.

I tried to wiggle my toes, but I couldn't.

"Look what I have," said Evan.
He showed me a shiny key.
"Mom can't pick me up this year
because she's working. After school,
my babysitter and I will stop
by your dad's grocery store
to say hi and get a snack.
Then we will walk home together.
I'm big enough to have my own house key,
and she has one too."

Charlie opened his Bug World backpack.
He pulled out two notebooks
and a new pencil box.
Inside was a ruler, colored pencils
and markers, #2 pencils, and a gum eraser.
"I hope we're in the same class
this year," he said.
"Me, too," I said.
"But even if we're not, we'll still be friends."

Next, we went down the slide.

When Dad came over, I told him,

"My toes hurt. I think my shoes are too small."

Dad felt my toes.

"We need to go shopping," he said.

On the way home, we stopped at the shoe store.

Guess who was there?

Mrs. Madoff!

"Hi, Nicholas," she said. "All set for school?"

"You bet," I said. "I can't wait!"

"Neither can I," she said.

On the first day of school, I was ready.
Best of all,
Charlie and I were in the same class.